$14.95

**PEOPLE
WHO MADE
A DIFFERENCE**

LECH WALESA

Titles in the
PEOPLE WHO MADE A DIFFERENCE
series include

Louis Braille
Marie Curie
Father Damien
Mahatma Gandhi
Bob Geldof
Mikhail Gorbachev
Martin Luther King, Jr.
Abraham Lincoln
Nelson Mandela
Ralph Nader
Florence Nightingale
Louis Pasteur
Albert Schweitzer
Mother Teresa
Sojourner Truth
Desmond Tutu
Lech Walesa
Raoul Wallenberg

North American edition first published in 1992 by
Gareth Stevens Children's Books
1555 North RiverCenter Drive, Suite 201
Milwaukee, Wisconsin 53212, USA

This edition copyright © 1992 by Gareth Stevens, Inc.; abridged from *Lech Walesa: The leader of Solidarity and campaigner for freedom and human rights in Poland*, copyright © 1990 by Exley Publications Ltd. and written by Mary Craig. Additional end matter copyright © 1992 by Gareth Stevens, Inc.
All rights reserved. No part of this book may be reproduced in any form or by any means without permission in writing from Gareth Stevens, Inc.

Library of Congress Cataloging-in-Publication Data

Angel, Ann, 1952-
    Lech Walesa : champion of freedom for Poland / Ann Angel, Mary Craig.
      p. cm. — (People who made a difference)
    Includes index.
    Summary: Presents events in the life of the Polish union organizer who after years of non-violent fighting with the government became president of his country.
    ISBN 0-8368-0628-X
    1. Walesa, Lech, 1943- —Juvenile literature. 2. Presidents—Poland—Biography—Juvenile literature. [1. Walesa, Lech, 1943- 2. Presidents—Poland. 3. Labor unions—Biography. 4. Poland—History.] I. Craig, Mary. II. Title. III. Series.
DK4452.W34A54   1991   943.805'6'092—dc20
[B]   91-50539

For a free color catalog describing Gareth Stevens' list of high-quality children's books, call

1-800-341-3569 (USA) or
1-800-461-9120 (Canada)

PICTURE CREDITS
Associated Press 7, 10, 49; Camera Press 6-7, 21 — Dirk Buwalda 22 (lower left), Jan Hausbrandt 27, W. Krynski 36-37, Bob Wales 45 (upper); Mary Craig 11 (upper); Dachau Museum 5; Janina Jaworska, Warsaw 4; Keston College 11 (lower), 57; David King 13; Popperfoto 54; Tom Redman cover illustration; Rex Features — Laski/Setbourn 40, Laski 44, 50; Frank Spooner — Bogdan Borkowski 18 (lower), 20, Mark Bulka 31, 32, 33, 34, 37, 42, Thierry Campion 45 (lower), J. Czarnecki 24, 25, 43 (both), 58-59, Gamma 51, Chip Hires 55, Klahr 22 (lower right), Kok 18 (upper), 46 (upper), 52-53, François Lochon 16-17, 19, 38, 39, 48, Remis Martin 22 (upper), N.S.P./Gamma 56, Jean-Paul Paireault 28, Simon & Francolin 15, Bob Wales 41; Voice of Solidarity 46 (lower). Map drawn by Geoff Pleasance.

Series conceived by Helen Exley
Editor: Amy Bauman
Editorial assistant: Diane Laska

Printed in MEXICO

                1 2 3 4 5 6 7 8 9 96 95 94 93 92

**PEOPLE
WHO MADE
A DIFFERENCE**

*Champion of
freedom for
Poland*

LECH
WALESA

Ann Angel

Mary Craig

Gareth Stevens Children's Books
MILWAUKEE

Opposite: Concentration camps were set up in Poland for all who opposed Germany's Nazi party or who were considered racially inferior. The camps were the scene of much slaughter. Lech Walesa's father died as a result of his years in a concentration camp. This painting shows Polish prison workers.

Nazi occupation

In September 1939, World War II began as Nazi Germany and the Soviet Union invaded Poland. The two forces then split Poland between them, beginning one of the worst periods of persecution that Poland's people have ever known.

Germany's leader, Adolf Hitler, wanted Polish lands for Germany, but he had little use for the Polish people. He urged his followers in occupied Poland to kill "all men, women and children of Polish race or language."

It was a dark time for the Polish people. Their blond, blue-eyed children were kidnapped off the streets and sent to Germany. There, the children were raised as "Aryans" — members of the "master race" of which Hitler dreamed. Thousands of Poles were shot. Others became laborers. "The Poles will work," said Hans Frank, governor of occupied Poland. "And in the end they will die. There will never again be a Poland."

Into this misery, Lech Walesa was born in the little Polish village of Popowo on September 29, 1943.

Below: A Nazi guard kicks a prisoner. This sketch is reproduced from a picture that now hangs in the Dachau Museum, Germany.

Right: Poles captured by the Germans are shot in Ustron, Silesia, 1939. Eleven million people were killed in Poland during World War II.

Opposite, below: Polish youngsters build a road in Germany under the watchful eyes of Nazi soldiers. Many Polish girls and boys were taken from their families and forced to work for the Nazis.

"Poland [became] the home of humanity's holocaust."
  Norman Davies, from God's Playground: A History of Poland, Volume II

When the Germans invaded Poland, Walesa's father, Boleslaw (Bolek), and his mother, Feliksa, were living with their three small children in a stone hut. Their part of Poland had become part of the German Reich. Polish places soon had German names. Polish flags, schools, and libraries were destroyed. Germans took over Polish lands, while the Poles became farmhands or were sent to work in German military forts along the rivers.

Bolek Walesa, like many Poles, helped the Polish resistance movement, called the Home Army partisans. Members hid until night, when they came out to find food and do what they could to damage German operations. People sheltering the partisans risked their lives. Many were shot or hanged for this crime.

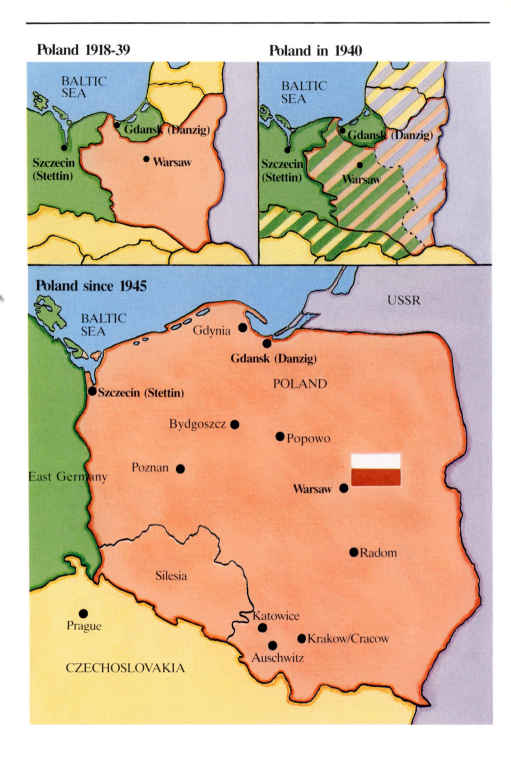

Walesa's sister, Izabela, was nine years old at the time. She brought supplies to the men who met secretly in the Walesa cowshed. In 1943, just before Lech was born, the men of Popowo were caught. Bolek Walesa and his brother Stanislaw were arrested along with the others.

Many of the men arrested in that roundup were beaten to death during the first few days. Bolek survived, but he was sent away to labor for the Nazis, digging trenches and building bridges. His pregnant wife was left to look after the farm and three children.

Into this unhappy situation Lech was born. The war would rob him of many things, including his father, who died in 1945 just after the war ended.

A country destroyed

One-fifth of Poland's people were killed in the war. Almost 90 percent of those killed were shot or hanged, or died in concentration camps. Poland's fortunes didn't improve after the war. As the Soviets pushed the Germans out, their Red Army moved in. Nazi rule was replaced by Communism, headed by Joseph Stalin in Moscow.

Poland and the other Eastern European countries of Hungary, Romania, Bulgaria, and Czechoslovakia all became part of the new Soviet empire. Stalin's takeover of Eastern Europe

"The world has learned little to this day of Russia's part in the crucifixion of Poland."
Mary Craig, from The Crystal Spirit

Opposite: Poland is seen through the years. After centuries of occupation, Poland enjoyed independence from 1918 to 1939 (top, left). In 1939, in a secret pact, the Soviet Union and Germany divided Poland (top, right). At the end of World War II, Poland was Poland again. But it then became part of the Communist-held Eastern bloc (bottom).

Harvesting in peace, 1945. By this time, the Germans had been driven out of Poland and the war was over. Here on a farm near the former border with East Prussia, farm workers gathered the first harvest in six years.

"In one sense we had nothing, but you can't judge poverty by material standards. We weren't well-off, we didn't have television, or even radio, but we had books, and the whole world of nature was open for us to read."

Lech Walesa

---

marked the start of what came to be known as the Cold War between the Soviet Union and the West. This period of tension and competition was not to end until 1989.

A difficult childhood

The Walesas were more concerned with survival than with politics. A year after Bolek's death, Feliksa married his brother, Stanislaw. The couple soon had three children of their own. This meant a total of seven children and two adults now shared the tiny cottage, which had an earthen floor and no electricity.

Stanislaw didn't have much luck farming, so the family had very little money. Although they didn't starve, their meals consisted of potatoes, milk, and noodles. Everyone worked hard, including the children, who tended animals and sowed, weeded, and harvested fields before and after school.

The children attended school in the village of Chalin. There, Lech, whose surname *Walesa* means "a restless spirit," lived up to his name. He argued with the teachers a lot and got into trouble. "They taught us communism," he said, "and I didn't pay attention. . . . The trouble was that if I could see that something or other was white, no one was going to persuade me that it was really black."

At home, Lech often fought with Stanislaw, who was a harsh stepfather. He was influenced instead by his mother, Feliksa. She was a gentle, deeply religious woman who was fascinated with history and current affairs. All day long she scrubbed, sewed, and cooked for the family. In the evening, she still had the energy to read to her children from the Polish classics.

Even as a boy, Walesa saw how the Polish people had suffered. So when the Poles revolted against the Communist regime in June of 1956, twelve-year-old Lech understood why. Stalin had died three years earlier, but the system had remained. Thousands of workers in the city of Poznan went on strike. They marched in the streets, calling for "bread and freedom." The Polish government

*Above: The two-room Walesa house.
Below: Crosses in Poznan remind everyone of the workers' uprising in 1956.*

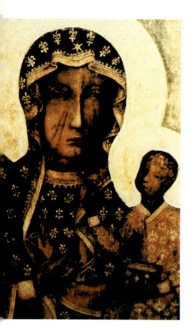

In 1655, an invading Swedish army was about to take over Poland. The Poles felt only a miracle could save them. A miracle did. When the Swedes reached the city of Czestochowa, they found a handful of Polish soldiers surrounding the picture of the Black Madonna. After blockading the city for forty days, the enemy retreated. Amazed by this event, the nation expelled the Swedes and proclaimed that the Blessed Virgin was thereafter "the Queen of Poland."

called out troops, and many people were arrested, wounded, or killed.

This protest brought political change to the country. A new government formed under Wladyslaw Gomulka, the leader of the Polish United Workers' party. Reforms were promised. The people called this time their "Springtime in October" and hoped that things would improve. Sadly, life continued as before.

Trade school

By 1959, sixteen-year-old Lech was ready to get away from farm life. In the 1950s, many Polish peasant boys felt the same and flocked to the shipyards of Baltic Sea towns such as Gdansk and Gdynia. That year, Lech enrolled at a trade school in Lipno, a town near Popowo.

Each week he spent three days training in a workshop. Another three days he studied math, technical drawing, physics, and general subjects such as language and history. History was always Lech's weak spot. He thought it had little to do with real life.

Walesa is remembered as a quiet, hard-working student. The school's director considered him an excellent organizer, recalling that whenever Walesa was put in charge of a project, he needed no help from the teaching staff.

After he left the trade school in 1961, Walesa, now eighteen, spent two years as

This Soviet propaganda poster by artist Dimitry Orlov shows a member of the Communist Red Army stomping on "Polish capitalist oppressors." Across centuries, Poland had been attacked by Russia from the east and Germany from the west.

a mechanic. He mended electric machinery at a state agricultural depot near his home before being drafted into the Polish army.

He enjoyed military service and soon became a corporal. "I didn't have any trouble from the men," he recalled. "I managed to get further with them through good humor and jokes than others did through shooting at them."

He did so well that he thought about making the army his career. But in 1965, he returned home to begin work in another state agricultural depot near Popowo. At work he was known as "golden hands" because of his skill at repairing everything from a rusty tractor to a television. But even with such skill, he couldn't earn a decent wage. "I was twenty-four and had achieved nothing of any significance," Walesa recalled. "Somehow I knew in my bones that I was in the wrong place."

Hardship in Gdansk

One day, Walesa went to the railroad station and bought a one-way ticket to Gdansk on the Baltic coast. As a child, he had been on a trip to Gdansk, and it had left him with a desire to be near the sea. He recalled "something vast, stretching out endlessly — possibly freedom."

In Gdansk's huge Lenin Shipyard, he found work as a ship's electrician. The shipyard was very different from the rural setting he had left behind. But he soon settled into his new life and for the first time had a taste of freedom.

His working conditions, however, horrified him. Most of the men began work at 6:00 A.M. and worked for eight or more hours with only a fifteen minute break. There was hardly any safety equipment and no place to wash. The men worked outside in all weather and often went home soaked to the skin. A worker's health was always in danger.

Many workers realized the situation was bad but felt powerless to change it. The trade unions existed, but their

---

"Our shipyard looked like a factory filled with men in filthy rags, unable to wash themselves or urinate in toilets. . . . You can't imagine how humiliating those working conditions were."
Lech Walesa

purpose was to make the workers work faster and produce more for the same small wage.

Walesa began to see that the workers always lost out. With that knowledge came an irresistable urge to change things. Before long, that urge would become a commitment.

The students protest

In 1968, students all over Western Europe began protesting for more power and an end to the Communist way of doing things. In nearby Czechoslovakia, the government of Joseph Stalin had been overthrown. Alexander Dubcek, a more liberal leader, replaced him.

Polish students also began protesting, but their demands were basic. They wanted the right to hold and express opinions. They wanted an end to official censorship that kept them from saying, reading, or writing what they wanted. When the government would not hear them, riots followed. Thousands of students were arrested, hurt, or expelled from their universities. Thirty thousand students were sent into exile.

Meanwhile, the attempt to establish better conditions in Czechoslovakia ended when the Soviets and their allies invaded and restored order by force. Polish troops were used to end the revolt. Polish workers strongly disapproved of

Workers at the Lenin Shipyard in Gdansk. The shipyard employs fifteen thousand people. It builds between twenty and thirty ships a year. Each of these ships weighs about 200 thousand tons.

"I am a radical but not a suicidal one. I am a man who has to win because he does not know how to lose. At the same time, if I know that I can't win today because I don't have a good enough hand, I ask for a reshuffling and then check whether I have got a better hand. I never give up."

— Lech Walesa

using Polish troops against Czech rebels although they hadn't said much about the fate of the Polish students.

At public meetings, authorities tried to stir the Polish workers' anger against the students. There, the authorities began calling the students "spoiled brats" and "hooligans." They blamed the young people for every wrong in the country, including the workers' low wages.

Some workers accepted this. Lech Walesa did not. He and a few friends

argued that if the students and other protesters were being persecuted by the government, the workers should support them. It was his first plea for solidarity — but it failed.

Marriage and commitment

March 1968 marked Walesa's first steps into politics. It also marked the moment he met and fell in love with the woman he would marry. One day, he caught sight of nineteen-year-old Danuta Golós

The presence of Soviet tanks on Polish soil reminded the Polish people of the ever-present threat of military punishment if they stepped out of line.

17

Right: Shortages of almost everything meant that store shelves were often empty.

Opposite: People rose before dawn to get a good place in line at the butcher shop. After this, there were lines to stand in at another shop for bread, soup, or soap.

Below: Danuta Golós and Lech Walesa were married on November 8, 1969. She found him to be "different from other men, both in the way he behaved and in his whole attitude to life."

in the Gdansk flower shop where she worked. He asked her out, beginning a one-year courtship. Like Walesa, Danuta Golós came from a large, rural family but dreamed of a better life.

They were married on November 8, 1969. "We were terribly poor," Danuta remembered of the time. "But life was very good. I could say it was the happiest time of my life because Lech and I were always together."

But in general, life for the Polish people had become a constant struggle with food shortages, price increases, and low wages. Then, on December 12, 1970, the government announced that food and fuel prices were being raised again. Wages, however, were not.

The workers had had enough. Two days later, one thousand shipyard workers surrounded the Communist

> "For us, December 1970 was dark and lonely; ours was the sort of cause that is lost in advance..."
>
> Lech Walesa, from his autobiography, Path of Hope

party headquarters in Gdansk. The workers demanded an end to price increases. The authorities ordered the workers back to work.

On December 15, shipyard workers called a strike. Twenty-seven-year-old Lech Walesa was elected to the three-man strike committee. With Walesa as leader, three thousand workers stormed police headquarters. The authorities declared a state of emergency.

On the morning of December 16, as a new shift of men arrived, they found the yard ringed by army units and tanks. No one thought the army would attack the workers, but it did. As the workers left the shipyard to join the demonstrations, shots rang out. Four men were killed.

In response, workers throughout the region put down their tools. Ten thousand workers attacked and set fire to the Communist party building. Officials were beaten by the crowd. The battle raged all day long. By evening, six people had been killed and three hundred injured.

The December 1970 Massacre

The following day, December 17, 1970, will never be forgotten in Gdynia, another Baltic town. That day, workers and police engaged in bloody battles. Hundreds of people were arrested; many others were killed. Those who were

A miserable lunch of one sausage left shipyard workers hungry. This only added to the horrid working conditions in the shipyard. This gave Walesa the "urge to go out and change things."

killed were buried secretly at night so that relatives would not find them.

Walesa felt guilty about the massacre for years. He felt he had failed the workers and brooded over what he might have done differently. But one day, he knew, he would get another chance, and when that day came, he would be ready.

Unkept promises

The anguish and rage of the Polish people spelled the end for Wladyslaw Gomulka, the first secretary of the Polish United Workers' (or Communist) party and, in effect, the leader of the country. He was replaced by Edward Gierek.

Lech Walesa was one of three shipyard workers chosen to meet with Gierek shortly after he came to power. Poland's new leader managed to calm the workers. He claimed he understood the people's problems and asked them to work with him. They agreed.

At first, things did seem to improve. Even Walesa was enthusiastic. In later years, he admitted he was easily fooled. The early seventies were the years of détente. During this period, relations between the Soviet bloc and the West relaxed. Edward Gierek put a lot of money in new industry, updating and importing machinery on credit from the West. Goods produced in the new high-

Poland's primitive living conditions and constant shortages made life especially hard for Polish women. Their lives amounted to hours of waiting outside shops, hunting, bargaining, bartering, and housework.

Far above: The Poles were tired and frustrated with their poor living conditions. Above and right: The Polish government deprived farmers of supplies and technical aid. Most of them used horses, had no tractors, and found it difficult to obtain loans.

tech factories were exported to the West in exchange for the money that Poland needed to pay its debts.

Gierek promised "a little Fiat car for everyone and decent housing for every family." Suddenly, the Poles, who had had few luxuries, were able to buy things such as washing machines, radios, refrigerators, and televisions.

But it did not last. In 1974, the price of Arab oil shot up, resulting in a recession in the West. People stopped buying Polish goods, and Poland's economy suffered. Suddenly, to buy the most basic items such as toilet paper and toothpaste, the people had to spend hours in lines outside shops. Food was in short supply again, too.

At the Gdansk shipyard, Gierek's changes hadn't amounted to much. The yard had been modernized to increase production, but the workers' health and safety still weren't concerns. Wages had increased slightly, but working hours were longer.

Walesa speaks out

Walesa realized that shipyard managers were getting rid of workers who had been active in the December 1970 strike. He himself was being given the worst jobs and was never promoted.

By 1976, he could no longer stand it. He had to speak out. At a shipyard union

"I have always believed that I am the steward of whatever talents I've been given and have to use them to the best effect. . . . I wasn't prepared for great tasks, but life put me in this situation and I have had to do what I can with it."

Lech Walesa

23

> *"There was this deadening conviction that there was no point in doing anything, since nothing could ever be changed."*
> — Lech Walesa

meeting, he criticized the union for being a "rubber stamp" for the party and accused Gierek of failing to keep any of his promises. The workers cheered, but authorities did not. A few days later, Walesa was fired from the shipyard. Luckily, he found a new job overhauling cars at the Zremb Building Company. Thirty-two-year-old Lech Walesa had taken an open political stand. He had begun the work that would lead to the Solidarity movement.

The riots of 1976

Discontent rumbled through the country. In June 1976, Gierek announced that food prices had to go up and the rate of wage increases had to slow down. Workers at the Ursus tractor factory in Warsaw responded by tearing up the tracks of the Paris-Moscow railroad line, which ran through the factory. Then they set up a blockade so that no trains could enter or leave Warsaw. Meanwhile, workers in the town of Radom set fire to the Communist party headquarters.

The government reacted violently. Police clubbed workers, arresting some — whether or not they had been in the demonstrations — and killing others. Within a few hours, the prisons were bursting, and special courts were set up to hand out sentences based on false evidence. The workers of Radom and

Like this mother and her children, a third of Poland's population were living in poverty by the 1970s.

Ursus were called "enemies of society," and all Poles were asked to report such "troublemakers" to the police.

In Gdansk, Walesa realized that to survive, the workers must unite. He believed then, as he said in 1981, that "with strikes, we shall all simply destroy ourselves. We must all stand together." Only when people united, Walesa believed, would they be allowed to express their grievances and think for themselves. In his view, a life without such freedom was scarcely worth living.

Standing for human rights

Others in Poland were reaching the same conclusion. Among them was the Workers' Defense Committee, or KOR. This group was set up to aid workers unjustly punished after the riots. The KOR collected proof of police brutality and legal corruption and reported its findings in underground newspapers.

Gierek angrily ordered an all-out war on the KOR group. Many members lost their jobs. Their apartments were searched and looted. Others were attacked or even killed by the police or by "unknown assailants."

KOR members refused to be frightened. They realized that fear was the authorities' greatest weapon. "Once you can rise above the fear," said Jack Kuron, a leader of KOR, "you are a free

By the late 1970s, Poland was almost bankrupt and faced constant food shortages. The little available food was usually of poor quality. The poor diets that resulted caused much illness among the working people.

> *"People began to understand that they could gather together in large numbers for religious purposes, and no harm would come to them, no matter how many riot police surrounded them. They learned to keep calm, to carry on praying or doing whatever they had to do, and to pay no attention to those who might want to stop them."*
> — Bohdan Cywinski

human being." So they acted as though they lived in a free society. They lectured, taught, and signed their names to articles they wrote.

The public began to sympathize with the KOR group. At the same time, the Roman Catholic church, to which most Poles belonged, was speaking out for human rights and asking for social reform. One passionate voice was Karol Wojtyla, cardinal of Cracow. Soon, he would become Pope John Paul II.

A call for free trade unions

Lech Walesa was among the workers who organized the Baltic Committee for Free and Independent Trade Unions on April 29, 1978. Avoiding the police, members met in small groups, always in a different place and at a different time.

Through its magazine, *Coastal Worker*, the group produced a "Charter of Workers' Rights," signed by sixty-five activists, including Walesa. The charter told workers to band together in independent trade unions. Only then, it said, would they find the strength to challenge authorities.

The police began to follow Walesa everywhere. They often jailed him for a day or two but did not charge him. This did not stop Walesa from distributing leaflets and copies of *Coastal Worker* in the streets. At work, he talked openly of

The Polish pope, John Paul II, received a hero's welcome when he visited his homeland in 1979. On a visit to the concentration camp at Auschwitz, the pope laid a wreath on the memorial to the millions of Jewish victims murdered in the camp.

the need for a workers' organization that would defend human rights.

Not surprisingly, Walesa was fired again. Angry co-workers threatened to strike. Walesa asked them to be cautious. "We're not strong enough yet," he advised. "But the time is coming when we shall be stronger than they are, and that's when we shall act."

Not everyone shared Walesa's hope, but they shared his frustration. As Danuta Walesa said, "I don't want my

"From the difficult experience we call Poland, a better future can emerge, but only if you yourselves are honorable, free in spirit and strong in conviction."
Pope John Paul II, June 1979

children to have the same sort of life Lech and I have had. I wish they could live in a country that was free, without this awful feeling of helplessness."

A few bright spots

To the delight of the Poles, Cardinal Karol Wojtyla of Cracow became Pope John Paul II in October 1978. When he visited his homeland in 1979, he was given a hero's welcome. His visit boosted the people's morale and gave them a new, stronger sense of solidarity.

Poor housing added to Poland's terrible living conditions in the 1970s. Young people sometimes waited fifteen years for a three-room apartment in a bleak building. Because of the long wait, two or three generations often lived together in crowded apartments.

Also in 1979, Walesa found work with Elektromontaz, a firm producing electrical equipment. By this time, the police followed him everywhere. They wanted to know what he had done, to whom he had spoken, and what they had discussed. As people learned of the harassment and Walesa's patience with it, more and more of them began to support the idea of free trade unions.

Remembering the massacre

Walesa was determined to be present for the 1979 anniversary of the December 1970 Massacre. The day before the anniversary, policemen arrived at the factory to remove him by force. Fellow workers smuggled Walesa out in the trunk of a small car.

Walesa hid until the evening of December 16, when he joined seven thousand people at the shipyard gate in a memorial service. There, he climbed onto someone's shoulders to make a speech. He held the crowd spellbound as he spoke of the part he had played in the tragic events of 1970 and of the hopes that Edward Gierek had betrayed. He also begged everyone to organize into groups for their mutual protection.

The authorities acted swiftly. The next day, fourteen men were fired at Elektromontaz, including the company's best electrician, Lech Walesa. With a

"It was bad enough that there was next to nothing in the shops. But to raise the price of nothing took the people over the top."
Tim Sebastian, correspondent, speaking on BBC-TV, 1980

> *"The clerk who dismissed me said: 'Anna, it's terrible what they're doing. I had to take two pills before I could bring myself to give you your cards.' I replied: 'Then why have you done it?' 'They'll sack me if I don't do as they ask,' she said, 'and then someone else would come in and do it.'"*
> — Anna Walentynowicz

sixth child on the way, Walesa was once again out of work.

Poland was almost bankrupt. Food supplies had dwindled, and the lines outside shops had grown longer. Women rose before dawn to line up at the shops by six. Entire families shared tiny apartments. As conditions grew worse, the government assured people that everything was splendid. Most Poles despised the party and longed for honesty and openness.

Shipyard strike

The Walesas' sixth child, a girl named Ania, was born in 1980, at almost the same time as Solidarity. Just as the birth began, the police hauled Walesa away for questioning once again. When he returned, the baby had been born. Walesa's anger grew to think the system had so little regard for human dignity.

All over the country that summer, strikes broke out in protest against food shortages and rising prices. At the Gdansk shipyard, workers were also enraged by the firing of Anna Walentynowicz, just five months before she was to retire. Walentynowicz was a crane operator who also happened to be a dedicated champion of workers' rights.

On the morning of August 14, members of the Young Poland Movement distributed leaflets asking the

Lech Walesa (seen in the middle of the picture) was the workers' leader during the historic 1980 factory solidarity strike. This strike changed the face of Poland.

workers to strike for the reinstatement of both Walentynowicz and Walesa.

Walesa went to the shipyard, expecting to be arrested on the way. The shipyard director was standing on a bulldozer, arguing with the men. He had almost talked them into going back to work when Walesa arrived.

"Remember me?" he yelled. "I gave ten years' work to this shipyard and then was fired. Well, I'm here to tell you we're not going to listen to any more of your

During the strike in 1980, this Mass was attended by 1,500 striking workers and their supporters on the other side of the gate. The Roman Catholic church had emerged as a powerful champion of human rights in a country where no political opposition was allowed.

lying promises." With that, all talk of returning to work was abandoned.

A sit-in for solidarity

Walesa called for an immediate sit-down strike. He also persuaded the workers to elect a committee to work out demands. The workers wanted Walentynowicz and Walesa rehired, no punishment of the strikers, a pay raise, and permission to build a monument for the victims of the 1970 massacre.

By the next day, several factories from Gdansk and Gdynia had joined the strike. It was the start of a full-scale showdown with Poland's leaders. From this small strike grew a solidarity strike that would affect most of Poland.

As the strike grew, so did the list of demands. The new list had twenty-one items and included a demand for an uncensored press, the right to strike, freedom of expression, and the right to free and independent trade unions.

The strikers' demands reflected the nation's misery over food shortages, poor medical care, and inequalities that existed between the privileged and the majority of the people. The workers sought a fairer deal and an end to lies and half-truths.

As strikers from hundreds of factories joined the shipyard workers, the strike became a workers' solidarity strike. It grabbed the attention of the entire world. Foreign journalists and television crews poured into Gdansk.

Families and friends talked to the strikers through the gates, decorated with pictures of the pope and fresh red and white flowers, symbols of the Polish flag. As food was passed in to workers, a team of women cooked and prepared in a makeshift kitchen. The strikers slept on the grass, cement floors, air mattresses, and tabletops.

"People came from the city by bicycle or on foot; they baked and cooked and carried food and cigarettes. Horse-drawn carts began arriving at the docks laden with potatoes, cabbages, cheese and apples from the farmers. There was even a cartload of pigs...."
Lech Walesa

Walesa has never seen himself as anything but a typical Polish worker. In his own words, "Everyman's story is my story."

Walesa takes charge

Walesa was solidarity's hero. Although the strike was led by a committee and was receiving advice from KOR leaders, it was Walesa who seemed to best understand the strikers. He had a natural authority and an understanding of the workers' needs and feelings. Walesa spoke a language the strikers could understand. He was one of them.

Meanwhile, in industrial cities around Poland, workers followed Walesa's example and set up their own factory committees. Smaller strikes began erupting all across the country.

Edward Gierek realized he was losing control of the situation, but would not, at first, talk with an independent strike committee organized by factory workers. He sent minor officials to talk separately with representatives from each of the factories, hoping to divide them. But it did not work. In the end, Gierek sent one of his best negotiators, Deputy Prime Minister Mieczyslaw Jagielski, to talk with the whole strike committee.

Jagielski and his team arrived in Gdansk on August 23, 1980. As their bus reached the shipyard, twenty thousand angry workers surrounded it, shouting, "Get out and walk," and "On your knees to the workers." Only Walesa, who had come to greet the delegates, was able to calm the workers.

The world watched in August 1980 as government officials traveled to Gdansk to talk with striking Polish workers. Everyone hoped that the talks would settle the strike.

Talks begin

In a glass-walled room, Jagielski came face to face with Lech Walesa. Hordes of workers, journalists, observers, and photographers peered through the glass while every word was relayed by loudspeakers to the world.

"These strikes must stop," Jagielski began.

"Well, that depends on you," Walesa answered. "Where do you stand on our twenty-one demands?"

"Allow me to make a few general points," bluffed Jagielski.

Walesa didn't budge. "No, I want a solid answer point by point."

Those listening could hardly believe their ears. In Lech Walesa they had a spokesman who could stand up to a party bigwig from Warsaw. Even so, Walesa's task was not easy, and days later, they were still bargaining. Jagielski had agreed to some demands, but he refused to allow free trade unions.

Meanwhile, the Soviet government was threatening to invade Poland if "the leading role of the party" in Polish affairs was undermined. Ignoring this threat, the miners of Silesia and the steelworkers of Nowa Huta went on strike and formed their own factory committees.

By then, the shipyard strikers were very tired. They were also worried about actions the Polish government might

Nationwide support for the strike was almost total. Many people described Solidarity, saying, "We were together at last."

take next. Few could be sure that security forces would not move in and start shooting, just as they had in 1970.

Solidarity!

Walesa did what he could to keep them calm. His reputation grew as the workers saw that he spoke honestly in a nation whose ruling party had for so long been dishonest. Walesa was offering the moral leadership for which Poland was hungry.

By August 30, it was clear that an agreement would be reached. That night, excited workers carried Walesa shoulder-high to the main gate. They wore stickers displaying the new SOLIDARNOSC logo. Soon, its English

translation, "Solidarity," would be known worldwide. This was the name of the first free trade union in the Soviet bloc. Nations would watch with fascination as the Poles continued to fight for the right to organize unions.

The Gdansk Agreement was finally signed on Sunday, August 31, 1980. That day, Walesa spoke from the heart when he said: "We may not have got everything we wanted, but we got the most important, our independent self-governing trade unions. That is our guarantee for the future. We have fought for all of you. And now I declare this strike to be over."

Applause from the hall was echoed by cheering from outside. Walesa signed

On August 31, 1980, Lech Walesa signed the Gdansk Agreement.

37

the agreement. Grinning to the waiting workers, he shook both fists in the air like a winning boxer.

In signing the Gdansk Agreement, the Polish government showed an amazing change of attitude. It was unbelievable that such an agreement could be made in a country that had been Communist for thirty-five years. If the promises were kept, the workers had won the right to strike, a higher minimum wage, and improved welfare allowances. Also, censorship was to be used only for security purposes, and the state radio would broadcast Mass to the nation every Sunday. From now on, managers in all state enterprises were to be chosen because they could be trusted to put the party's interests first. But even at this moment of joy, Walesa knew that the agreement was only a beginning.

Polish students plastered posters and political graffiti on walls all over Warsaw. It was one of the only ways they could protest.

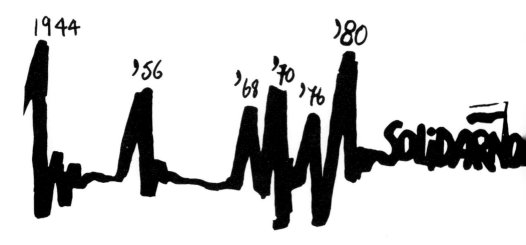

Walesa's supporters enthusiastically greet him in Warsaw.

The ink was hardly dry on the paper when Edward Gierek resigned. He was replaced by Stanislaw Kania, a liberal Communist. Almost overnight, unions sprouted up across the country, and before long, Solidarity had ten million members. The people burned with enthusiasm as Solidarity began planning for Poland's transformation. They loved their new freedom.

"It was the dawn of a new era," wrote Walesa. "We felt that after so many years of living upside down, we were at last beginning to walk the right way up."

Unfortunately, it wasn't like that everywhere. In some places, the authorities tried to limit the powers of new unions. They refused to recognize them and threatened Soviet intrusion.

"During the sixteen months following August 1980 . . . we were able to take charge of our own problems instead of being helpless dupes . . . in the power struggles of others."

Lech Walesa, from his autobiography, Path of Hope

> *"Nobody wanted him [Lech Walesa] not to be a leader. In a country where lies and censorship still hold sway, we had to have a name which stood for honesty and truth."*
>
> *Solidarity member*

The troubleshooter

Every day, many letters and hundreds of people arrived at Solidarity's Warsaw office. And it was all for Lech Walesa. According to a woman who worked with him at the time: "They brought him their marriage problems, housing problems, everything. No one gave him time to think, and everyone expected him to work miracles."

Walesa enjoyed the fuss and was flattered by the admiration, but he hated sitting in an office. He had a passion for people and enjoyed speaking to them. He liked holding them spellbound with his enthusiasm and honesty.

But now that change was a possibility, not everyone wanted Walesa as leader. Some of those on the Baltic Committee for Free and Independent Trade Unions didn't. They thought Walesa was ill-informed and not revolutionary enough

Walesa is shown here with KOR advisor Bronislaw Geremek. At the peak of Solidarity's power, everyone wanted to hear Walesa speak.

in his demands. They asked him to step aside for someone more knowledgeable. But Walesa knew the workers wanted him. He was not about to step down.

It wasn't easy to lead such a diverse movement. Many of the workers were eager to get rid of those who had made them suffer: the government officials who had been feathering their nests at the public's expense, the dishonest factory bosses, and others. Walesa also had to assure Poland's leaders that Solidarity had no intention of overthrowing the government. On the contrary, Solidarity members saw the organization as existing simply to protect the workers' rights.

The regime strikes again

Sadly, Solidarity's moment had come before people were able to cope with freedom and democracy. Walesa was well aware that the unions had no clear policies and that they wanted too much too quickly. They needed time to sort themselves out, but time was something they did not have.

The Polish government took advantage of this unreadiness. Its leaders were not about to keep the promises they had made in August — not unless forced to. They made Walesa, as chairman of the Solidarity National Commission, fight every inch of the way.

"Our situation is like that wall over there; if anyone takes just one more brick out of it, it'll fall on top of us. The most important thing right now is for us to get together and create a really effective trade union."
Lech Walesa

Lech and Danuta Walesa sleep on a bus taking them from one meeting to another. The demands on Lech's time were overpowering, and his private life suffered.

He had to threaten a nationwide strike before Solidarity was even registered as an independent trade union.

Many workers were disappointed by the effort it had taken to get Solidarity registered. Taking matters into their own hands, they went on strike. Walesa was kept busy dashing across the country, stopping wildcat strikes as they erupted.

The Gdansk Monument

The authorities did keep one promise. They allowed the people to build a monument to the workers killed in the 1970 Massacre. On the tenth anniversary of that day, government officials, military people, foreign diplomats, clergy, and 150 thousand Poles stood in driving sleet. They had come together to unveil the monument near the Gdansk shipyard.

But the impressive ceremony was only a truce. The government continued to make and break promises, and the workers continued to strike. In February 1981, Stanislaw Kania named stern-faced General Wojciech Jaruzelski the new prime minister.

Matters came to a head in March 1981 in the small town of Bydgoszcz. Here, police broke into a Solidarity meeting and beat some of its members. People were outraged. Solidarity, feeling that its existence was threatened, began to plan a general strike. Even Communist party

The three steel crosses of the Gdansk Monument stand just outside the Lenin Shipyard. A black anchor hangs from each cross as a symbol of hope. The monument itself honors the workers' rebellions of 1956, 1970, and 1976.

Strikes spread across Poland. The top picture shows the nation's capital, Warsaw, crippled by a transportation strike. At left, a glass factory, closed by strikers, stands empty.

Lech and Danuta have eight children: four boys and four girls. Two of the girls, Maria Wiktorja and Brygyda, were born after this photograph was taken. The older six include Bogdan, Slawek, Przemek, Jarek, Magda, and Ania.

members within Solidarity supported the proposed strike.

But Lech Walesa did not share the enthusiasm. To him it seemed that the country was about to plunge into civil war. Polish Cardinal Stefan Wyszynski also believed this and supported Walesa's attempts to stop the strike.

Shortly before war could erupt, Walesa reached an agreement with the Polish government. He then presented the agreement to Solidarity's National Commission. They were furious that he had not consulted the group earlier. Walesa was not disturbed by the criticism. "I will not let things come to civil war," he insisted. "I know how far we can go with our demands. And I know in what country we live, and what our realities are."

He was, of course, referring to Poland's close ties to the Soviet Union. As the Soviets moved to surround Poland with tanks and warships to the north and east, people feared that they would soon invade. Walesa had not been prepared for this possibility. It looked like the end for Solidarity. In his heart, he knew that the government was preparing for a war to the death.

Meanwhile, Walesa set off to encourage worldwide solidarity. His first visit was to the Vatican to meet Pope John Paul II and to talk with the Italian

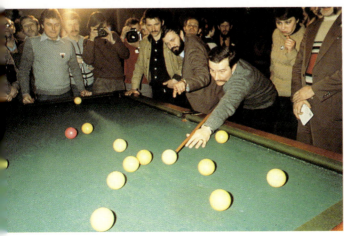

Above: Leading Solidarity takes its toll on Walesa.
Left: Even Walesa's rare off-duty moments were no longer private. Reporters and television crews followed him everywhere he went.

Jaruzelski declared martial law in 1981, crushing the Poles' active resistance. After this, the people used quieter methods. Above: A postmark, with its V-for-Victory sign, barbed wire, and black anchor, showed the Poles had not given up. Below: A poster calls for Walesa's release.

trade unionists. After that, he went to France, Switzerland, Sweden, and Japan, "to bear witness to our movement before the whole world." Everywhere he went, he spoke of the need for international solidarity among workers.

Anger and despair

In Poland, the shops were almost bare now. Potatoes had nearly disappeared. Meat, butter, sugar, rice, and flour were strictly rationed and often unavailable. Even hospitals were without food. Patients had to rely on whatever relatives could scrape together.

As the Poles got hungrier, they also grew angrier. They were tired of the shortages and the endless hours of waiting in lines. People often slept on the roadside all night so as not to lose their places in lines outside shops.

Food wasn't the only problem. By this time, money had no value, and bartering was the only way to "buy" anything. Factories, meanwhile, had run out of parts, raw materials, and fuels. As the country slid into chaos, the government didn't even pretend to govern.

At Solidarity's first National Congress in Gdansk in September 1981, delegates decided it was time to act. Against Walesa's advice, they called on workers in the Soviet Union and Eastern Europe to form free trade unions.

Walesa insisted that the only way to bring change was for Solidarity, the church, and the government to get around a table as equal partners and discuss a plan of action.

Jaruzelski comes to power

Solidarity's outburst angered the politicians. One week later, party leader Stanislaw Kania was replaced by General Wojciech Jaruzelski. The general now became head of state as well as prime minister and chief of the armed forces.

On November 4, 1981, Lech Walesa met with General Jaruzelski and church leader Cardinal Jozef Glemp. When the meeting produced no results, the government stepped up its media attacks on Solidarity. Later that month, the specially trained riot police, the Motorized Units of Civil Militia, called ZOMO, raided a sit-in by students at the Warsaw Fire Academy. As Solidarity once again threatened a general strike, Walesa hastily called his executive staff to an emergency meeting in Radom.

The meeting room was bugged. Three days later, Walesa's voice was heard on Warsaw Radio stating that civil war could not be avoided. Walesa protested that his words had been edited and that it was the government that wanted civil war. The government-controlled media turned on him, calling him a "big liar."

"I do what I have to do, regardless of consequences. Obviously, some people will not like it and may decide to put me behind bars. But it doesn't matter what they decide. The most important freedom is inner freedom, and in that sense I am the freest man in the world."

Lech Walesa

The specially trained riot police called ZOMO met all Solidarity protests with riot vehicles, tear gas, and fire hoses.

On December 11, Walesa opened a meeting of Solidarity's National Commission in the Lenin Shipyard. "We do not want confrontation," Walesa insisted. But Solidarity's commission had had enough and voted for a nationwide strike on December 17. Solidarity members were still meeting when they heard reports of troop movements and telephone line cut-offs.

A nation at war

On Saturday, December 12, 1981, General Jaruzelski struck. Solidarity's buildings were seized, and its leaders were rounded up by the police. As tanks and riot vehicles rumbled through the streets, the police arrested Solidarity members all over Poland.

General Jaruzelski took military control of Poland. On Sunday, he told a stunned nation that he had installed a Military Council of National Salvation to save Poland from chaos. The Poles believed such military control, or martial law, was the same as declaring war on Poles. From then on, they referred to this experience as "the war."

Martial law

Under martial law, a curfew was in force from 6:00 P.M to 6:00 A.M. People on the streets during this time were arrested or sometimes shot. Travel outside Poland was not allowed. Inside the country, no one was to use private cars, and public transportation was restricted. Riot vehicles and tanks were everywhere.

All gatherings except church services were banned. Trade unions and student groups were suspended. Workers who continued to support Solidarity were fired from their jobs; student supporters were expelled from school.

Everybody over age thirty was to carry identification and be prepared to be searched. After this, the police were constantly making identity checks. Telephone lines were monitored or simply cut. News broadcasts once again were controlled by the government.

In the evening of December 1, 1981, people gathered near the Gdansk Monument to mark the eleventh anniversary of the December Massacre. ZOMOs broke up the ceremony using tear gas and fire hoses.

Opposite: On May 1, 1982, nearly 100 thousand Solidarity supporters gathered to demand that Walesa be freed.

Below: Danuta (holding Ania in a 1982 photo) showed herself to be strong and capable. While Lech was in prison, for example, she had to be both mother and father to her children. "She's more of a hero than I am," Walesa has said.

Nonviolent resistance

Early December 13, the police arrested Lech Walesa. They sentenced him to a year-long prison sentence in Warsaw. Later that day, the authorities tried to persuade him to appear on television to reassure the Polish people. He refused.

But Walesa did smuggle out an appeal for nonviolent resistance against the ZOMOs. Although Solidarity had had no time to organize resistance, some workers were resisting. At the Wujek mine near Katowice, for example, eight miners were killed defending the mine.

The Poles responded to Walesa's appeal in imaginative ways. They stopped buying official newspapers and watching television. They listened to sources such as Radio Free Europe to gain a true picture of how things were.

The silence of Lech Walesa

Walesa was kept in solitary confinement. Still, he was not treated as poorly as many of Solidarity's members were. Many of these people were held in rat-infested cells without proper medical care or hygiene. Walesa was probably treated better because Jaruzelski hoped to win Walesa's cooperation. He even offered Walesa control of the new official unions that were to replace Solidarity.

Walesa stood firm, refusing to recognize the new unions. He insisted

that no agreement was possible with the military until martial law was lifted and Solidarity leaders released from prison. Without his colleagues, he said, he had no right to speak. He chose to remain silent, and his silence became the symbol of Polish defiance.

Prison gave Walesa time to plan and taught him patience. "If we fail in what we set out to do, then we have to start again," he decided. "Nothing is ever final. Life is all fresh starts."

Outside the prisons, Jaruzelski dealt ruthlessly with all opposition. On May 3, 1982, Poland's national day, ZOMO squads attacked demonstrators with missiles and tear gas. On the August anniversary of the Gdansk Agreement, reports came in from all over the country of police shooting at demonstrators. Even women and children were abused.

Solidarity worked hard at being nonviolent. On May 13, 1982, traffic throughout the country came to a halt as people poured into the streets in support of Solidarity. Wearing Solidarity badges, protestors stood still with hands lifted in the V-is-for-Victory salute. The ZOMOs responded violently, with gas, clubs, and water hoses.

Toward the end of 1982, General Jaruzelski declared Solidarity illegal and said it did not even exist. Although the freedom that Solidarity brought no longer existed, Solidarity was still alive as an underground organization. And as Walesa asked, the Poles remained true to Solidarity's belief in nonviolence.

A man of no importance

Perhaps to prove that Solidarity didn't exist, the authorities set Walesa free in November 1982. They said he was a man of no importance. The Poles thought differently. When Walesa arrived home, thousands of people were waiting for him in Gdansk. With banners and cheers, they greeted him joyously.

For a while after his release, Walesa led a quiet life. But when several Solidarity leaders went on trial, Walesa came back

> "In sixteen months this revolution killed nobody.... This extraordinary record of nonviolence, this majestic self-restraint in the face of many provocations, distinguishes the Polish revolution from previous revolutions."
> Timothy Garton Ash, from The Polish Revolution: Solidarity

In November 1982, Walesa was released and went home to Gdansk and his family.

"We had, during those five hundred days, set in motion an alternative society, while the whole of Poland awakened from its long slumber."

Lech Walesa, from his autobiography, Path of Hope

---

to life. Already he had given interviews to the foreign press. Now he began secretly meeting with Solidarity advisors. Each day, there were more people to see and more letters to answer.

From then on, police followed Walesa wherever he went. His apartment was bugged, and the police knew everything he did. "I am the freest man in the world," he told visitors. "If you're free inside yourself, you're free no matter what the authorities decide to do."

Perhaps to restrict his schedule, authorities returned Walesa to his old job at the Lenin Shipyard in April 1983. When he rose at 5:00 A.M. for work, he would find security police waiting outside his apartment. If they had fallen asleep, he would rap on the car and shout, "Wake up! Time to get going!" One winter morning, he even persuaded them to help him start his car!

A country in darkness

Martial law officially ended in July 1983, but nothing much changed. The government and people grew farther apart by the day as the poor conditions continued to get worse. Hospitals were so crowded that children slept in corridors waiting for vacant beds. Nurses washed soiled sheets and clothing in basins, and orderlies mopped floors without disinfectants. Surgeons

had to use disposable items more than once. Truckloads of food, clothing, and medical supplies sent from Western countries kept the Polish people alive.

For five years, Poland remained in this darkness. Visitors described the country as a nation of "no-hopers," in which the only cure was to get out. Many Poles, especially the young, decided to do just that and immigrated to the West. Despite the horrid conditions, anyone who opposed the government ended up in prison — often without a trial. Some rebels were even murdered. Among these were Father Jerzy Popieluszko, murdered in 1984, and Father Stanislaw Suchowolec, murdered in 1989.

Walesa returned to his job as an electrician. The man who had been the "uncrowned king of Poland" was happy to be an ordinary person once again.

"I have always been an ordinary worker. . . . That doesn't mean that I have no ambition to improve myself. But to the end of my days I shall be a working man."

Lech Walesa

A glimmer of hope

The only glimmer of hope in this dark time came in October 1983, when Lech Walesa won the Nobel Peace Prize. When the award was announced, Walesa was picking mushrooms with friends. Shouting in triumph, the group quickly returned to Gdansk to find an excited crowd of foreign news teams and Poles waiting to see Walesa.

Lech did not go to Norway to accept the award. He was afraid that if he left the country, he would not be allowed to return. Danuta went in his place. She even read his Nobel acceptance speech. In it, Lech claimed that the award belonged to all of Solidarity because the organization had remained nonviolent even when violence was used against it. All his life, Walesa said, he had been surrounded by "violence, hatred, and lies." The lesson this had taught him was that "we can effectively oppose violence only if we do not resort to it."

Walesa's Nobel Prize focused the world's attention once again on Poland, but it had little effect on the country's leaders. They continued to say that Walesa was a citizen of no importance.

Lech Walesa did not go to Norway to collect his Nobel Peace Prize. He asked Danuta and their son Bogdan to go in his place. The Walesas were afraid that if Lech left the country, the government would not allow him to return.

The scene changes

By 1988, the government was paralyzed. Wage increases could not keep up with skyrocketing prices. The government began to fear massive protests from the people. Finally, in August, strikes broke out in Gdansk and other industrial areas.

Walesa calmed the strikers and again asked the government to bring back Solidarity. Finally, he was allowed to argue Solidarity's case on television with the head of the party-approved trade unions. He made the Communist party leaders look weak.

By 1989, the government had run out of answers. Jaruzelski finally turned to Walesa — the "man of no importance" — for help. At a conference, Walesa described the discontent of the Polish people. The two sides bargained for weeks but finally reached an agreement.

By this agreement, Solidarity was made legal again. The agreement also set up a new parliament and allowed for free elections. Now a person no longer needed the Communist party's approval to win an election. The first free election was held in June 1989. Of 360 seats in the lower house, Solidarity agreed to run for only 161. They won all 161. Of the 100 seats in the Senate, Solidarity members won 99. The election proved that Solidarity had the people's support.

Walesa becomes president

On December 9, 1990, Poland gained the opportunity to become a free market nation when Lech Walesa was elected

Jerzy Popieluszko, a Roman Catholic priest, worked hard in support of Solidarity. He became a voice for the hopes and fears of the people during martial law. Secret police murdered Popieluszko in 1984, causing worldwide outrage.

president of Poland by an overwhelming majority of people. On December 12, he announced that he would step down as leader of Solidarity, pledging that as president he would make peaceful changes in Poland.

On December 22, 1990, the forty-seven-year-old shipyard electrician took the oath of office in Warsaw. He was surrounded by family, friends, and coworkers. Walesa knew that Poland

Solidarity was banned in 1981, but the people did not forget. They waited, hoped, and worked for Solidarity and the freedom it had promised. By 1990, their efforts paid off. Solidarity was legal again and Lech Walesa was president of Poland.

would need strong and wise leadership because the country was still in turmoil. Walesa promised this leadership while moving toward change. Today the people of Poland rejoice even as they struggle because they realize that a democracy is really theirs.

"Lech Walesa has made humanity bigger and more inviolable. His two-edged good fortune is that he has won a victory which is not of this, our political, world. The presentation of the Peace Prize to him today is a homage to the power of victory which abides in one person's belief, in his courage to follow his call."
Egil Aarvik, Chairman of the Norwegian Nobel Committee

To find out more . . .

Organizations

Throughout the world, unions represent groups like steelworkers, graphic artists, people who work for the government, and many others. Listed below are just some of the organizations that deal with labor, unions, and the issues that affect them. Write to these organizations if you want to learn more about labor and government, the Solidarity movement, or the conditions for workers throughout the world. When you write, be sure to include your name, address, age, and a stamped, self-addressed envelope for a reply.

Education Department
   International Confederation
   of Free Trade Unions
37-41, rue Montagne aux
   Herbes Potageres
B-1000 Brussels, Belgium

Friends of Solidarity
c/o Chris Michejda
21 Frasta Court
Rockville, MD 20850

International Labor
   Organization
4, rue des Morillons
CH-1211 Geneva, Switzerland

Solidarity International
c/o Solidarity Support
Committee of Rhode Island
340 Lockwood Street
Providence, RI 02907

Books

The books listed below will help you learn more about Poland, about labor unions in the United States, and about people in union history. Check your library or bookstore to see if they have them.

Heroes of American Labor. Linda Morgan (Fleet Press)
Poland. Carol Greene (Childrens Press)
Poland. Cass R. Sandak (Franklin Watts)
Poland: Land of Freedom Fighters. Christine Pfeiffer (Dillon Press)
Stolen Years. Sara Zyskind (Lerner Publications)
Take a Trip to Poland. Keith Lye (Franklin Watts)

The Unions. Leonard E. Fisher (Holiday House)
We Live in Poland. Ewa Donica and Tim Sharman (Franklin Watts)
The Worker in America. Jane Claypool (Franklin Watts)

Magazines

The following magazines will give you more information about careers and events around the world that affect the lives of working people. Check your library to see if these magazines are available or write to the addresses listed below to get information about subscribing.

Career World
General Learning Corporation
60 Revere Drive
Northbrook, IL 60062-1563

Current Events
Field Publication
4343 Equity Drive
Columbus, OH 43228

Faces
20 Grove Street
Peterborough, NH 03458

List of new words

Aryans
   Originally the name given to all descendants of a people called Indo-Europeans, who, in prehistoric times, spread from central Asia into southern Asia and Europe. In the nineteenth century, the idea arose that the Aryan race was superior to all others and that Germanic people were the "purest" of the Aryan descendants. Although scientists rejected this idea, Adolf Hitler seized upon it. Hitler also narrowed the term so that it came to mean specifically people with blond hair and blue eyes — traits common among the Germanic people. It was Hitler's dream that members of this "master race" would rule the world.

BBC
   The British Broadcasting Corporation, the government-chartered broadcasting network in the United Kingdom.

bloc
A group of people, parties, or nations united by a common interest. This term has often been used to refer to the Communist countries that separated the Soviet Union from the West. These buffer states were known as the Eastern bloc.

censorship
The act of controlling communication. Governments that censor watch all forms of communication (radio, television, newspapers, etc.) and remove anything that they consider objectionable or do not want the public to know.

cold war
A state of tension and competition that exists between power groups. This term often refers specifically to the period of this kind that existed between the Communist countries of Eastern Europe and Asia, led by the Soviet Union, and the democracies of the West, led by the United States. This cold war began after World War II and did not end until 1989.

communism
A political system based on the belief that a nation's people as a whole — not individuals — should own the resources used to produce goods. In theory, communism's goal is to distribute wealth equally and provide for everyone's needs.

détente
A period when tensions between countries are lessened.

Hitler, Adolf (1889-1945)
Born in Austria and known for his extreme anti-Semitism, Hitler became the leader of Germany's Nazi party in 1925. He gained even more power in 1933 when he became both Germany's chancellor and its dictator. While in this position, he started World War II when he ordered an attack on Poland in 1939. Hitler killed himself in Berlin in 1945 when it became clear that Germany had lost the war.

Holocaust
The Jewish name for the period from 1933 to 1945, during which Hitler put into action his plan to kill all Jews and members of other minorities in Europe. The word Holocaust means "great destruction or loss of life."

KOR (Komitet Obrony Robotników)
A group set up in 1976 to provide legal and financial aid to workers who were unjustly punished by the police. In English, the group's name is the Workers' Defense Committee.

logo
An abbreviation of the word *logotype*, the symbol that an organization or publication uses to represent itself.

manifesto
A public statement outlining the beliefs, policies, and goals of an organization, usually a political organization.

Marxist
A person who follows the ideas of two German philosophers, Karl Marx and Friedrich Engels.

master race
(*see* **Aryans**)

Nazi
A member of Adolf Hitler's political party, the National Socialist German Workers' party, which was founded in 1919. The Nazi party came to power in Germany when Hitler became chancellor and dictator in 1933.

Nobel Prizes
Sweden's much-respected yearly awards, given for outstanding work in the areas of chemistry, economics, literature, medicine, and physics. Alfred Nobel was the founder of the prizes, which were first awarded in 1901.

partisan
   A member of a rebel group working in secret — often behind enemy lines — against an enemy. Often, partisans are the people of a conquered country resisting their invaders. Many Poles were part of the Home Army partisans during World War II.

Polish United Workers' party
   The ruling Communist party in Poland, formed in 1947. In Poland, it is usually referred to simply as the Party.

Red Army
   The former name for the army of the Soviet Union. The army was renamed the Soviet Army in 1946.

regime
   The system of government. This term is also used to refer to the government that is in power.

Reich
   The name given to the government of a German empire. Adolf Hitler's Nazi regime, which held power from 1933 to 1945, was called the Third Reich.

Solidarity
   The name of the independent trade union set up in Poland. Solidarity was formed in 1980 and led by Lech Walesa.

Soviet Union
   Another name for the Union of Soviet Socialist Republics, or the USSR.

Stalin, Joseph (1879-1953)
   A Russian leader who became the dictator of the Soviet Union in 1924. Stalin changed the country from an agricultural to an industrial society. He also transferred industry and agriculture from private to government ownership.

ZOMO (Zmotoryzowane Oddzialy Milicji Obywatelskiej)
In English, "Motorized Units of Civil Militia" — an organization of 25,000 to 30,000 specially trained riot police. The ZOMOs were used in Poland to spy on Solidarity members and their families.

Important dates

1918   After World War I, Poland once again becomes an independent nation. By this date, Poland's history had been marked by many invasions as more powerful neighbors constantly conquered and claimed its territory.

1939   **September 1** — Germany, under Adolf Hitler, invades Poland from the west. World War II begins.
September 17 — The Soviet Union invades Poland from the east. Both the USSR and Germany occupy the country for the remainder of the war.

1943   **September** — The invading Germans take Boleslaw Walesa, Lech Walesa's father, prisoner. Boleslaw, also known as Bolek, is sent to a labor camp, leaving his wife, Feliksa, and three children behind.
September 29 — Lech Walesa, the fourth and last child of Bolek and Feliksa Walesa, is born in Popowo, Poland.

1944   The German army is driven out of Poland by Soviet forces. Poland is under Soviet domination.

1945   **March** — Bolek Walesa is freed and returns to Popowo.
May — Bolek Walesa dies.

1946   Feliksa Walesa marries Stanislaw Walesa, Bolek's brother.

1947   Poland is declared a communist people's republic.

1948   The Polish United Workers' party is formed.

1959	Lech, aged sixteen, starts a three-year course at the trade school in the nearby city of Lipno.
1963	Lech serves two years in the Polish army.
1967	**May** — At the age of twenty-three, Walesa begins work in the Lenin Shipyard in Gdansk, a city on the Baltic Sea.
1969	**November 8** — Lech Walesa marries Danuta Golós.
1970	**December 12** — The Polish government announces drastic increases in fuel and food prices. **December 14** — In protest, shipyard workers in Gdansk and Gdynia go on strike. Troops called in to halt the strikes fire on workers. **December 17** — Days of fighting result in the December Massacre. This day, in open battles, Polish troops kill striking workers.
1976	**February** — Walesa loses his job at the shipyard after speaking out against the Polish authorities.
1978	**April 29** — Workers, including Walesa, set up the Baltic Committee for Free and Independent Trade Unions. **October** — Cardinal Karol Wojtyla of Cracow becomes Pope John Paul II.
1979	**June** — Pope John Paul II visits Poland.
1980	**August** — Walesa calls for a sit-down strike at the Lenin Shipyard in Gdansk. **August 31** — The Gdansk Agreement is signed. Independent trade unions become legal. **November** — Solidarity is registered as an independent trade union, the first in a Soviet-controlled country.
1981	**March** — Security police beat up Solidarity members

during a meeting in the small town of Bydgoszcz.
September — Solidarity holds its first National Congress.
October — Stanislaw Kania resigns as party leader and is replaced by General Wojciech Jaruzelski.
November 4 — Walesa, Jaruzelski, and Cardinal Jozef Glemp meet for talks.
December — General Jaruzelski imposes a state of martial law. Across Poland, Solidarity's leaders are arrested, and Walesa begins a year's imprisonment.

1982   **October** — Solidarity is outlawed.
November — Walesa is released from jail.

1983   **April** — Walesa returns to work at the Lenin Shipyard.
July — Martial law ends. As the country tries to return to "normal," its economy struggles. Living conditions for the mass of Poles grows worse.
October — Lech Walesa wins the Nobel Peace Prize.

1989   As Poland falls into chaos, the workers grow tired of living in poverty. As a last effort, the government asks Lech Walesa for help in calming the workers.
February 6 — Walesa opens talks in Warsaw between the Polish government and Solidarity.
April 17 — Solidarity is legalized again.
June — Solidarity wins 99 out of 100 Senate seats. Allowed to run for only 161 of 360 seats in the lower house, Solidarity wins all 161.

1990   **December 9** — Lech Walesa is elected Poland's president in the country's first general elections since World War II.
December 12 — Walesa steps down as Solidarity's leader.
December 22 — Walesa takes the oath of office in Warsaw, Poland. He is officially the country's president.

Index

Aryans 5

Baltic Committee for Free and Independent Trade Unions 26, 40

censorship 15, 38
Cold War 10
concentration camps 5, 27

December Massacre 20-21, 29, 49
Dubcek, Alexander 15

Eastern bloc 9-10, 21

Gdansk Agreement 37-38, 52
Gierek, Edward 21, 29, 34, 39
Glemp, Josef 47
Gomulka, Wladyslaw 12, 21

Hitler, Adolf 5
Home Army partisans 6, 9

Jagielski, Mieczyslaw 34, 35
Jaruzelski, Wojciech 42, 47, 48, 49, 50, 52, 53, 54, 57
John Paul II (Wojtyla, Karol) 26, 44; visits Poland 27, 28

Kania, Stanislaw 39, 42, 47
KOR 25-26, 34, 40

Lenin Shipyard 14, 15, 42

martial law 46, 49-54
"master race" 5

Nazis 5-6, 9

Poland: gains world attention 33, 56; history of 12; holds free elections (1989) 57; occupation of 5-6, 9, 10; under martial law 49-54
Polish resistance 6, 9

Polish United Workers' party 12, 21
Popieluszko, Jerzy 55, 57
protests 11, 20, 24, 29-30, 38, 47, 49, 52; demands of protestors 15, 20; authorities' reaction to 11-12, 20-21, 24-25, 29, 34-37, 42, 47, 49, 52, 55

Solidarity: birth of 30-37; declared illegal 53, 59; and free elections of 1989 57; government attacks on 39, 42, 47, 48-50; legalized 37, 59; as underground organization 53-54
Soviet Union 9, 17; and strikes in Poland 35, 39, 44
Stalin, Joseph 9, 15
strikes 20-21, 30-31, 32-38, 42-43, 57; demands of strikers 20, 32-33; negotiations of 27, 34-37, 44, 47
Suchowolec, Stanislaw 55

trade unions, establishment of 26, 39, 46

Walentynowicz, Anna 28, 30-31, 32
Walesa, Boleslaw (Bolek) 5, 6, 9
Walesa, Danuta (Golós) 17-18, 27-28, 41, 44, 50, 56
Walesa, Feliksa 6, 9, 10, 11
Walesa, Lech: as chairman of the Solidarity National Commission 41, 44, 48; childhood of 9, 10-11; heads strike committee 20-21; as leader of Solidarity 30-36, 40-41, 57, 58; marriage and family of 17-18, 30, 44, 50, 56; meets Pope John Paul II 44; as president of Poland 57-59; wins the Nobel Peace Prize 56
Walesa, Stanislaw 9, 10, 11
Workers' Defense Committee (*see* KOR)
World War II 5-6, 9, 10, 27
Wyszynski, Stefan 44

ZOMO 47, 49, 50, 52